Where's
Buckshot?

First published in 2009
by Wayland

This paperback edition published in 2010

Text copyright © Mick Gowar
Illustration copyright © François Hall

Wayland
338 Euston Road
London NW1 3BH

Wayland Australia
Level 17/207 Kent Street
Sydney, NSW 2000

Series Editor: Louise John
Cover design: Paul Cherrill
Design: D.R.ink
Consultant: Shirley Bickler

A CIP catalogue record for this book is available from the British Library.

ISBN 9780750255523 (hbk)
ISBN 9780750255561 (pbk)

Printed in China

Wayland is a division of Hachette Children's Books,
an Hachette Livre UK Company

www.hachettelivre.co.uk

Where's Buckshot?

Written by Mick Gowar
Illustrated by François Hall

WAYLAND

Apart from Deputy Pete, Sheriff Stan's best friend was his horse, Buckshot.

Buckshot was the cleverest horse in Cactus Thorn. He could swim across wide rivers.

He could jump high fences.

He could even skate on frozen ponds.

Buckshot caught the Dalton gang
robbing Miss Candy's Sweet Shop.
He put them in jail.

8

"That horse is too clever by far,"
said Ma Dalton.

"Yes," said Dudley Dalton.
"I wish we had a clever horse
like Buckshot, and Sheriff Stan
had Dusty, our donkey."

"That's a brilliant idea, Dudley!"
said Ma. "As soon as we get out of
jail, we'll steal Buckshot, and Sheriff
Stan can have Dusty in his place!"

So, when Sheriff Stan let the
Daltons out of jail, Ma untied
Buckshot and led him away.
Buckshot neighed loudly.

Dudley tied Dusty up outside the
jail instead!

"Where will we hide Buckshot?"
asked Dudley.

"We'll make a secret camp in the woods," said Ma. "Sheriff Stan will never find us there!"

They tied a tent and bags of food
to Buckshot's saddle and off they
went to the woods.

They didn't see Buckshot leaving a trail of hay behind him!

"Sheriff Stan! Come quick!" shouted
Deputy Pete. "Buckshot's ears
have grown!"

"That's not Buckshot, that's Dusty
the Donkey," said Sheriff Stan.
"Someone's stolen Buckshot!"

"Oh, dear!" said Pete. "And someone's dropped hay everywhere, too. I'll sweep it up."

"No," said Stan. "It's a clue!
Follow the hay – the trail will lead
us to Buckshot!"

Sheriff Stan and Deputy Pete followed the hay trail all the way to the Dalton's camp.

Ma and Dudley were asleep in their tent. Buckshot was tied up outside. He was very pleased indeed to see Stan and Pete!

It was time to get their own back. Sheriff Stan and Deputy Pete tied all the tent ropes to Buckshot's saddle.

"Ready... steady... PULL!" shouted
Sheriff Stan.

"Help!" shouted Ma Dalton. "Wake up, Dudley! That horse has caught us again!"

"What? Where? Arrr..." groaned Dudley, and went back to sleep.

Buckshot pulled Ma and Dudley all the way back to Cactus Thorn jail. Dudley snored loudly all the way there.

"Hooray for Buckshot!" cried Deputy
Pete and Sheriff Stan.

"Hee-haw! Hee-haw!" laughed Dusty the Donkey.

START READING is a series of highly enjoyable books for beginner readers. **The books have been carefully graded to match the Book Bands widely used in schools.** This enables readers to be sure they choose books that match their own reading ability.

Look out for the Band colour on the book in our Start Reading logo.

The Bands are:

Pink Band 1

Red Band 2

Yellow Band 3

Blue Band 4

Green Band 5

Orange Band 6

Turquoise Band 7

Purple Band 8

Gold Band 9

START READING books can be read independently or shared with an adult. They promote the enjoyment of reading through satisfying stories supported by fun illustrations.

Mick Gowar has written more than 70 books for children, and likes to visit schools and libraries to give readings and lead workshops. He has also written plays and songs, and has worked with many orchestras. Mick writes his books in a shed in Cambridge.

François Hall loves the Wild West, but lives in a terraced 'ranch' down in the South. As well as being quick on the draw, he also designs knitting books. Cowboys often knitted on the homestead and poor Dudley has to wear very itchy underpants made by Ma Dalton!